To Christopher, Carlynne, and little Caleb—N.M.A.

For Ellie, Harry, and Jessie. Just one more became triplets—J.B.

Text copyright © 2007 by Nancy Markham Alberts
Illustrations copyright © 2007 by John Butler
All rights reserved
CIP Data is available

Published in the United States in 2007 by Handprint Books
413 Sixth Avenue
Brooklyn, New York 11215
www.handprintbooks.com

First Edition
Printed in China
ISBN: (10) 1-59354-195-3
ISBN: (13) 978-1-59354-195-8

2 4 6 8 10 9 7 5 3 1

JUST ONE MORE?

by Nancy Markham Alberts

illustrated by

John Butler

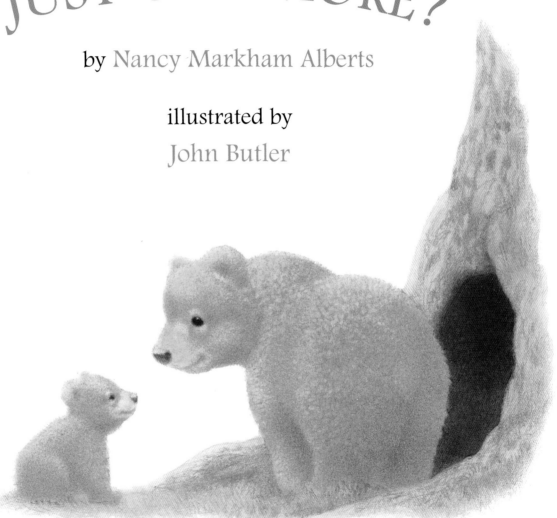

Handprint Books Brooklyn, New York

"Little One," called Mama. "Time for sleep."
"Not yet," answered the little bear. "I'm not tired.
Please, may I climb one more honey tree?"

"Yes, cub of mine, you may."

"Hurray!" said the little bear. He skipped to the highest honey tree and climbed up to the hole. No bees buzzed, so he scooped out a sweet-tasting pawful of honey.

Then as the sky turned deep blue, he climbed down and lumbered back to the clearing.

"Are you tired now?" asked Mama.
"Not yet," said the little bear. "Please,
may I catch just one more fish?"
"Yes, cub of mine, you may."
The little bear spun around.
"Hurray again! Hurray!"

He hurried through the
woods, kicking up leaves.

He slid down the hill and
splashed into the cold, cold stream.

"Brr!" He shivered as he waded
in deep. Way, way down in the water,
he caught a slow-moving trout and
ate it. Then he splashed out and ran
all the way back to the clearing.

Mama hugged him while his fur dried. By then the sky had turned orange. "It's warm in the den," she said. "Let's go inside."

"Not yet," answered the little bear. "Please, may I watch the sky turn just one more color?"

"Yes, cub of mine, just for tonight, you may watch until the sky turns gray."

The little bear leaned against Mama. He watched orange turn to pink and pink turn to purple and purple turn to gray and gray turn even deeper.

A round white light rose over the
trees. "Is that the sun already?" he asked.

"It is the moon," said Mama.

Then the little bear heard a long, lingering
whoo-whoo-whoo of an owl.

The little bear yawned.

"Time for sleep now," Mama whispered.

"Please, may I hear the owl again?"

"Yes, cub of mine, you may. But let's listen inside." She led him into the den where they snuggled on the soft dirt floor.

The little bear closed his eyes. Finally he heard the long, lingering call of the owl a second time. "Whoo~whoo~whoo."

His eyes blinked open. "Mama?" he murmured. "Why did you let me stay up so late tonight?"

"Because tonight we will sleep a very long, deep sleep. Hush, my little cub. Enough questions. Time to sleep now."

"Oh," said the little bear. "Goodnight, Mama. See you in the morning." He closed his eyes and drifted into sleep.

Mama nuzzled his ear and yawned. She whispered, "Goodnight, cub of mine . . .

. . . see you in the spring."